BLOOD ON POINSETTIA

A Serial Investigations Christmas Novella

Rhiannon D'Averc

First Edition November 2020

This is a work of fiction. Names, characters, businesses, places, events and incidents are either the products of the author's imagination or used in a fictitious manner. Any resemblance to actual persons, living or dead, or actual events is purely coincidental.

The author acknowledges the trademarked status and trademark owners of the following wordmarks mentioned in this work of fiction:

Craigslist: Craigslist, Inc

Facebook: Facebook, Inc

Twitter: Twitter, Inc

Also by Rhiannon D'Averc –

Standalone:

Boy Under Water - Dennis Nilsen: The Story of a Serial Killer

Serial Investigations:

Bloodless

Blood Evidence

Blood Alcohol

Blood Sucker

Blood Sport

Blood on Poinsettia (Christmas novella)

Blood Diamond

BECOME A VIP

If you love Serial Investigations, why not become a VIP? You'll get special goodies as well as access to books before they are launched to the general public. And you get to be part of the launch team for each book, ensuring that the series gains a wider audience!

To sign up, head to rhiannondaverc.co.uk/vip and enter a few quick details.

1 - RAM

The house feels so empty without Will.

When Alex leaves, after dropping me off from the hospital, it feels like I've come back to the wrong house. Not mine. There's a strange kind of atmosphere in the air that I can't put my finger on.

Maybe it's simply absence. We haven't been home for a while. Before this it was only me here on my own, and then Coil took us both, and then we were in the hospital, and no one came by to check on the place. Not that I even had the presence of mind to ask anybody to.

It looks like the site of a disaster: a place where people fled, leaving their lives behind. There are clothes left on the floor of my bedroom that have been there for weeks. Half the food in the fridge has gone off. My plates and cutlery from the day we were taken are still standing by the sink, waiting to be washed. I take one look at the things growing on the food scraps and throw them all wholesale into the binbag with the rest of the ruined things, then haul it outside for good measure to try to get rid of the smell.

I'm not supposed to exert myself, the doctors said, but I don't see what else I'm supposed to do. If I stop for even a second, I'll have to face it.

Face the fact that Will isn't here, and he won't be here for a long time, and I am on my own.

It's even worse than it was before. At least then he was somewhere I could reach him if I needed to. I was angry with him, but I could still go and see him, and that made it hurt less. Now, I know they won't let me see him until he's well enough to come home. That could be a very long time.

Months. He might not be home for Christmas.

That thought finally floors me, making me drop down onto the wooden boards of the living room, my back against the back of the sofa. From here I can see his room, the door still firmly closed. Half of his things aren't even in there. He took a bag with him when he went to stay with Harry, and Harry took it right over to the centre Will is in now.

I don't know how long I can bear to be without him. There's a racing in my chest, a tight feeling that won't go away. I'm afraid for him. If I'm not there to protect him, anything could happen. It's my job to make sure he's okay, and I can't do it from this distance.

I don't even know if he wants me to – if he'll want to give things a try when he comes out of rehab.

What if he comes home and tells me he can't stay with me? What if I'm too much of a trigger and he has to move out – for good?

All those things we said to each other in that cold, dark room – I meant them all. But did he, really? Or was it just the fear of imminent death talking?

I cover my face with my hands and scrub at my eyes, wanting this feeling to stop. This anxiety clutching at my chest, making me breathe hard and ragged, choking me. All I can think of is Will in danger, Will hurt and dying, Will needing me…

My head shoots up, a sudden and stronger fear gripping at me. He was watching us – Coil. He knew things. He was in this apartment.

I scramble to my feet and start searching, my hands shaking, careless in my haste. I knock over lamps, tear cushions from the sofa, pull down the light shades from the ceiling. I wrench open all of the kitchen cupboards one by one, pull everything out of them, rice scattering over the floor when I drop a packet off the counter.

Where are they? Where are the cameras? The microphones?

I can't believe for a single moment that Alex's team got them all.

The place barely looks disturbed – they didn't even get rid of the food - how could it be that they searched thoroughly? I picture DS Fox leading the search and calling it off after ten minutes, deliberately leaving us vulnerable. That man wouldn't lift a finger to help us even if it meant helping himself.

I don't even know how long I spend searching, tearing through the apartment in a frenzy, checking every inch of every room. Even his. Even though it wrenches my chest to step inside, even though I left it for last, I find myself rummaging through his drawers, throwing handfuls of clothes to the floor, flipping over picture frames to check for bugs, upending boxes of Korean face masks and pouring them onto the floor.

Nothing.

I falter, the adrenaline-fuelled energy of the search failing me. There's nowhere left to look. I've been *everywhere*. How can there not be anything to find?

I'm still in his room. In spite of myself, I sink down onto his bed, which still contains some small lingering trace of his smell. I think of him lying in bed in the hospital still, lying there alone, and turn my face to the pillow. I don't want to get it wet, but the tears fall all the same as I breathe him in, letting everything else fall away but him.

When I wake in the morning and look around, my muscles aching from falling asleep like that, I know I have work to do. I move methodically, keeping the curtains closed so no one can see in, putting one room and then another back together. I make lists of things I've broken, things I need to replace exactly the same so that everything is just how Will remembers it. I give myself things to do.

At night I sleep in his room again, in his bed, one of his jumpers from the washing basket pressed against my face. Before he comes home, I'll wash everything, tidy up. He'll never know I was here.

But I just can't bear to sleep alone.

TWO – WILL

I couldn't sleep, that first night. It was bad enough sleeping in the hospital, but there at least I was drugged. There was a kind of rhythm to the place at night too, the beeping of machines, the whirring of air conditioning, even the regular patter of shoes outside the door as a nurse did their rounds.

I got used to it. It was easy to fall asleep when you were so tired, when your body needed to recover. But as soon as I was well enough to leave, I went to the centre, and then everything was completely different.

I stayed awake, my eyes open, tracing invisible patterns across the ceiling. The thin curtains weren't quite enough to blot out the floodlights on the grounds, no doubt designed to ensure that none of us could sneak out during the night. Or run away. I wouldn't have blamed anyone who did. I wanted to be there, and I was having a hard time even still.

At some point, I must have drifted off. I knew I had, because I wasn't in the new room in the rehab centre anymore – I was back in there, in the abandoned factory, in the chamber Coil had prepared for us. I was sitting against the wall with my arms tied behind my back, unable to move, and Joe was in the cell with us, right in the centre of the room. He was there and so was Ram, and they were talking like friends.

I tried to tell him – to warn him. But when I opened my mouth, no noise came out. I was so weak that I couldn't even talk. I watched Joe reach out and touch Ram's shoulder, like a friend offering support, and I tried so hard to tell him. *Get away from him*, I wanted to scream. *It's Coil. Joe is Coil!*

Instead, I could only watch as Joe, Coil, leaned forwards, producing a knife from inside his jacket, his hands no longer tied. I could only watch as he plunged the knife deep into Ram, over and over again, staining his shirt red, his eyes wide open as he stared back at me accusingly.

"Why didn't you warn me?" he gasped, and then fell back, his throat open and glistening, Coil's knife slipping through the air beside it.

I woke with a start, sitting straight upright in bed, panting for breath. I clutched at my chest and wiped a hand over my eyes. It was just a dream. Ram was alright. He was alright, wasn't he?

Against all reasoning I got out of bed, rushing for the door, and out into the hall. I wanted to check on him, but – he wasn't here, I remembered. I wasn't at home. I was in the centre for my first night. I ran a hand over my face again, trying to breathe, trying to focus. I wasn't at home. I couldn't go and see him.

"What are you doing up?"

I turned, my heart pounding in my chest, to see a middle-aged woman in the hall behind me. I remembered her: Claire Swan, the staff member who had greeted me when I was being signed in. I had the vague feeling that she was in charge here, or at least high up.

"I…" I found my voice failing me, too many shocks in such a short space of time. The fear of the dream, the realization I had been asleep, the fear for Ram, the recollection that I wasn't home and couldn't go see him – and the fear of a stranger approaching me in a dark hall, only to find it was someone who was here to help.

"There's no exercising in your rooms," Claire said, snippily.

"I wasn't," I said, belatedly realising that I must have been dripping in sweat. "I was…"

"I can see what you've been up to," Claire said, shepherding me along towards my door. "You've got to stick to the rules here. They're in place for your benefit. If you don't, we may have to take drastic measures."

"I really wasn't exercising," I protested, re-entering my room. "I had a bad dream."

Claire paused as if trying to assess whether I was telling the truth or not. "You won't be homesick for long," she said. "It fades away when you start taking part in the activities and really becoming a member of the group. But we won't be able to help you if you don't help yourself."

"Understood," I said quietly, giving up on convincing her. She left me then, closing the door behind her, and I stripped out of my wet clothes and into something fresh, towelling off my face and hair. It was good to stay busy.

But once I'd done all of that, I was at a loss. I got back into bed and lay there, on the bumpy mattress with the unfamiliar sheets, staring up at the ceiling again. I wished Ram was there. It wasn't as though we slept in the same room normally, but over those few days in the cell – when we slept propped against one another for warmth – he became the only comfort I had to cling onto. It was hard to let that go.

I lay staring up at the ceiling and pictured him laying beside me, trying to feel his weight on the mattress making it dip. I pretended to myself that his arm was just a faint millimetre away from mine, just out of the range of where I could feel it, but close enough that all I had to do was move to touch him. I closed my eyes and lay like that, and when I opened them again I realised I'd managed to sleep through the rest of the night – and I had a busy first day ahead.

I couldn't focus on much as I prepared, dressing in one of my oversized jumpers for comfort and heading out to the first session: group therapy. Sitting in a circle and moaning about our lives. I wasn't looking forward to it. I wasn't much given to talking about myself at the best of times, and this was not the best of times – and these people were strangers.

Even worse, I saw as I joined them – most of them were teenagers. Young girls and women for the most part, with only a couple of other boys. All of them had to be younger than me. Most by more than a decade. I felt my heart sink, making me feel like I might throw up. I shouldn't be with a bunch of kids.

I shouldn't be so pathetic that I couldn't take care of myself more than a teenager could.

"Alright," another woman, one I hadn't met yet but who was wearing the uniform of the centre, said. "Let's take a moment to talk about our progress. Rachel, do you want to go first?"

And I sank against my chair, trying to make myself as small as possible in the hope that I might disappear, as a girl who couldn't have been more than thirteen years old with the body weight of a six-year-old started to talk.

3 – RAM

Why did I even bother?

I shake my head, angry at myself, angry at the world. I don't know what the point was. Yesterday it came in the post, and last night I wrapped it carefully in reindeer-printed paper. I spent extra time and care on the folds, making sure it was as neat as possible. I even bought tags so I could write his name, and then put it neatly in the corner of the room, where the tree would be if I had bothered to put it up.

And what was the point? It's not like Will can open it. Half of December is already gone, and he's been away for weeks already, and if he was coming home in time for Christmas I would have heard by now. I called the rehab centre and they told me they can't say anything about his progress because we're not family. It's bullshit.

We are family. We're the kind of family that you aren't born with – the kind that you choose. Whether we end up in a relationship after this or not, it doesn't change how close we are. The things we've been through together. For years we've been each other's support system, each other's crutch.

Maybe we failed at looking after each other – but that doesn't mean we aren't family.

I want a drink, and I want it bad. It's the only thing I can think of that will take away the ache. The hole in my very being that is left behind when Will isn't here. All I want to do is find out if he's okay. I can't call him, can't text or email him, can't go and stand outside Harry's place in a big coat with the hood up and watch until he comes outside so I know he's still coping. I can't find any way to contact him at all.

I think of madcap schemes – ways to sneak myself into the centre. I could pretend I need help with something. I could even check myself in for alcohol abuse, get into a programme. I know they offer them there. But I don't know if they let the different programmes mix. Probably not.

And I know I shouldn't do it anyway. The whole point of being no contact is to let the person who needs it heal. And I want Will to heal. I want him to be better, more than anything. If it meant that he would be okay, for good, then I would vow never to see him again. I would make that sacrifice for him. I just don't know if I would be able to carry on living afterwards.

You don't realise how much you relied on someone until they're gone. The dishes pile up in the sink, the clothes on my bedroom floor. The fridge is empty when I go to make myself lunch after waking up at one in the afternoon. I don't know how to break myself out of this cycle. I bought Will a Christmas present and he's not even going to be here to open it. I need a drink.

I need a drink.

I grab my leather jacket from the peg by the door and throw it on, searching in the inside pocket for my wallet. There's an off-licence down the road, but I already gave them my printed picture to put beside the till as a reminder not to serve me. I'll have to go a bit further. It doesn't matter. I can still get something. There's a pub not too much of a walk away – I could just go there.

I stop with my hand on the doorframe, freezing still. Will's shoes are still by the door where he last left them. Will wouldn't want me to do this. He would want me to stay strong. He needs me on the wagon so that when he gets back home, I can be who he needs me to be. I can support his recovery, rather than him having to worry about mine.

I take a breath and yank my phone out of my pocket, dialling Asra's number.

"Hello, Julius?"

"Asra," I gasp out, clinging onto her voice like a lifeline. "I need your help."

"What is it? Are you getting tempted?"

"Yeah. Yes. More than tempted. I was on my way out the door to go buy something. Please – I can't do this on my own – I can't take it."

"I'm on my way, honey. Go and grab some blankets so you can make up the couch for me later. By the time you've made your place suitable for a guest I'll be with you."

I close my eyes in relief as she ends the call and do as I'm told. It's funny: before this all happened I was never a fan of being given orders. But dealing with trauma, becoming an alcoholic – it changed me. I find that I like being told what to do. I can follow instructions, keep myself busy.

Asra is true to her word. Just as I finish clattering hastily-washed plates into the cupboard, I hear the buzz of our intercom and walk over to unlock the main door of the building for her. Just a few moments later she is standing in my doorway, hefting a small duffel bag over to the armchair and filling the room with her presence the way she does.

"Right, then," she says. "Have you finished cleaning up, or do you need a hand?"

I take a glance around. "I've finished?" I try.

"No, you haven't," Asra says, grabbing an empty pizza box from the coffee table and adjusting the edge of her hijab in a business-like manner. "Come on. Have you got any rubber gloves?"

When all the cleaning is finally done and the apartment practically sparkles, we collapse onto the sofa together, heads back against the cushions. "How did you let it get like this without calling me earlier?" she asks.

"I thought I was coping," I mutter stubbornly. "I've just…"

"What have you been doing all day?" Asra asks, shifting her head to look at me. "Are you working?"

"No," I say, roughly. I lean forward, elbows on my knees. I can't look at her. She's sitting how Will was that first time that we kissed. The ache in my heart for him is too strong to stand it. "I've mostly been sleeping. Watching films, TV shows. Anything to go somewhere else."

Asra's hand finds my forearm, squeezes sympathetically as I rub my hands over my face. "You need to get back to normal," she tells me. "Starting with a good daily routine, then some work if you can."

"I can't," I say. Unexpectedly, my voice cracks. "I can't sleep through the night. Every time I do, I'm there. Watching Will slowly dying before my eyes, unable to do anything about it. I couldn't even hold him. I couldn't get out. I knew he was dying, and I would be next."

"But you did get out," Asra says soothingly. She moves forward, rubs a slow hand across my back. "You did get out. You saved him – saved yourself. You stopped that man from hurting anyone else."

I can't stop the tears from escaping my eyes. "But it's like – there's no proof of that," I say, my voice splintering and breaking, shards of it lodging in my throat to ache and scratch. "Where is he? Where is he that I can look at him and know he's still safe? He's just – he's just gone, and I can't…"

Asra's hand continues to stroke my back, like a mothering touch. I get a jolt of homesickness. I never really had a mother like that. My parents spent my childhood partying. I'm longing for something I never had, I realise; no point in going home looking for it.

"He's safe," Asra says, her voice low and gentle. "He's as safe as he could possibly be. Not only did he survive, but he's getting help. They're making him better. Keeping him healthy so that he can come back to you."

"I know," I say, my voice muffled by my hands. The decorative rings I wear on odd fingers press cold metal against the skin of my face. "I know that. I want him to get better. But if I could just see him…?"

"I understand," Asra says, pulling me so that I lean my head down against her shoulder. "You want him to be better, but he's the thing that would make you better, too. You love him."

The words catch in my chest, even though I'm not even the one who said them. "I do."

"You see yourself as his protector." Asra pauses. "You never told me what happened to you in the US, what it was that made you start drinking. But I get the feeling that ever since then, you've wanted to protect Will as much as you could. Maybe for a while, you thought the best way to do that was to distance yourself from him, but you've changed. You're doing so much better. And you naturally want to look after him by keeping him close now – especially after what the two of you went through."

"I don't know when it's going to stop," I say, desperately. That tightness in my chest still hasn't gone away. "When I'm going to stop seeing it when I close my eyes. Every night, I – I sleep in his bed just to be close to him. To pretend I'm not alone. I can't bear being alone, As, I can't…"

"You're not alone," Asra says firmly. "We need to work on getting you better. On making you ready."

"Ready for what?" I ask. The tears are slowly stopping, but I don't want to move away from her. Just for right now, just for tonight, I want to be that little boy I once was, when it seemed like it was okay to ask for comfort. Before I decided to put on armour instead.

"For Will coming home," Asra says. "Because when he gets back here, when you're both healthy, you need to make a move on him. Let him know exactly how you feel. The two of you are meant to be together, but you can't do that if you're still falling apart."

"What if he doesn't want to be with me?"

Asra squeezes my arm. "He wants to be with you. And if he's not ready when he gets back, then you can still support him."

"You don't even know him," I huff, somewhere between a sob and a laugh. "You can't say that for sure."

"I know what you've told me," Asra says. She pauses meaningfully. "I know *you*, Julius. The way you look when you talk about him. The things you've done for him. Anyone would want to be with you. I mean, I'm almost jealous myself."

"You are?"

"Almost."

I smile. It gives me the strength to sit up, dash my hands across my face to scattering the lingering water, to breathe again. "For a second, I thought you were playing the long game."

"The long game?" Asra tilts her head questioningly.

"You know. Comfort me, tell me how great I am, get me to a good place so I can eventually see it was you who lifted me up all along. Then big Hollywood kiss scene, wedding finale, etc, etc."

Asra hits my arm. "It's nice to hear you sounding more like yourself, anyway."

I rub my arm in mock hurt. "I'm not that much better yet! There's no need for abuse."

Asra shakes her head with a smile. "If you think that was abuse, then wait and see what happens if you don't make an effort to get out of this slump," she says. "That's all it is, honey. A slump. You went through something awful and you need time to process it. But you won't achieve that hiding in here and sleeping all day. You need to get back to real life – and talk to me. Don't hold it in."

"Alright," I agree, taking a deep breath and sighing it out. "I will. I asked you here, didn't I?"

"And not a moment too soon, either," Asra says, looking around at the now clean and tidy living room. "Let's pick a movie to watch together, and I'll make dinner. And tonight, you're going to sleep in your own room."

I open my mouth to protest, but she cuts me off.

"You're not alone," she says. "I will be right out here on the sofa. You're going to go to sleep in your own room, tired enough from a good day with your friend that you won't have any dreams at all – good or bad. And in the morning, you're going to feel much better."

And when she says it so forcefully, her hazel eyes boring into mine from within the frame of her chestnut-coloured hijab, I almost feel as though she can't possibly be wrong.

FOUR – WILL

I picked at the food on my plate, wondering exactly how little I could get away with eating this time.

I should have set my benchmarks lower, I now realised. I should have refused to eat anything at all when I came in, so that even eating a small amount would have seemed like a victory. Then I wouldn't have them expecting me to finish a plate.

I didn't want to eat this meal, didn't want it at all. I'd been staring down at the insipid-looking Sunday roast for at least ten minutes already, managing to eat a few peas that escaped the lashings of gravy and nothing more. Sooner or later, someone was going to notice and force me to start eating real forkfuls. I just hoped it would be later.

"So, as I was saying," Claire announced, looking over the whole of the table from her position in the very centre. "We know it's hard for you to be away from home at Christmas, but it's important that you can celebrate it together here. Christmas is a time that can be very triggering for us, and if we ignored it completely, we wouldn't be giving you those skills that you need to take out into the world and deal with those triggering situations."

"What does that mean?" Jake, the only other male in the facility at the moment, asked. He was sitting a couple of seats down from me on the opposite side of the table, and I studied him for a moment. He was a teenager – maybe seventeen, almost a decade younger than me – with thick, curly hair that had a tendency to fall over his eyes. "What are we going to have to do?"

I appreciated his sentiment. I, too, was already feeling trepidation about what exactly this 'Christmas' was going to entail.

What was the point? It wouldn't be a real Christmas. Not without our families, the people we cared about. Ram was not so far away from me – in the same city – but he might as well have been on the other side of the world. I wasn't going to be able to see him.

"We're going to celebrate the day with some small gifts for one another, which we will be creating during our craft therapy sessions," Claire said. "We'll gather in the morning to hand out our gifts, and then in the afternoon, we'll join together for a traditional Christmas dinner."

There were groans around the table. I also felt my heart sink. My stomach roiled in protest at the thought of all that food. No – I couldn't. I couldn't eat that much. I'd told Ram I wanted to live, but that was all. I still didn't deserve to gorge myself like a pig. There was a difference between living and living recklessly. I had to keep at least some of the hunger: that was what made me real. Made me a good person. If I lost that, I would lose everything. I wouldn't deserve to live – and then I'd be stuck in this cycle again.

"After dinner," Claire said, trying to regain control of the table. "We'll be watching a festive film and spending some time relaxing together. No one is going to be exempt from attending."

"Not even non-Christians?" Fatema, a young Muslim girl who wore a hijab tight around her almost skeletal face, asked indignantly.

"Not even non-Christians," Claire confirmed. "I'm sorry, everyone, but this isn't a religious festival. It's an opportunity to try to regain some normality, as well as to deal with social situations in which you will be expected to eat larger quantities of food. We want you to celebrate and have a good time – but we also want to teach you how to live once you leave us. And ignoring a big occasion like this won't help."

I thought about Ram at home alone, and the other temptations that came along with celebrations like Christmas and New Year's Eve. Would he be tempted to drink? Would he fall? I wanted more than anything to reach out to him, to tell him to get me out of here. If I was with him at Christmas, he wouldn't need to drink. I could stop him.

I could get out of having to eat this meal.

I clenched my fists around my knife and fork so tightly that pain lanced through my palms, my short fingernails cutting into my skin. Around me, the girls were in an uproar, most of them talking over each other, each of them objecting vociferously to the proposed meal.

"That's enough," Claire said, cutting across all of them. "We hold the same Christmas celebration every year here. I won't hear any complaints from any of you, and you're not going to change my mind. Now, finish your food, all of you – and then you can get to bed."

I took a spoonful of mash, creamy and soft – which probably meant it had extra added calories in it – and forced it down. It was enough for me. I was done. I got up, scraping my chair back as I did so, ready to leave.

"Mr Wallace."

I looked up and found my way blocked by John, one of the counsellors here. He was massive, well over six foot tall with built muscles; he dealt with nutrition for the most part, and I could see that he knew exactly what to eat in order to not just stay healthy but to build the body you wanted. Not that I wanted a body like his. If anything, it went too far, to the point of being grotesque. There was an excess of him, like he was flaunting in our faces how little he cared about how much he weighed.

"I'm going to my room," I said, trying not to sound like a petulant teenager along with the rest of them. And failing.

"You haven't finished your meal," John said. He looked down at my plate with a raised eyebrow. "In fact, it looks as though you haven't started."

"I've been eating this whole time," I snapped. Somewhere, some small part of me knew that this was unreasonable. A handful of

peas eaten as slowly as was humanly possible didn't really consti-
tute a meal, and I knew that. But right now all I could understand
was that this man was trying to force me to eat, and if I wanted to
get away without having to do so, I needed to argue my way past
him.

"Sit down, Will," John intoned. His face brooked no argument.
"You need to set an example for everyone else here. You're a
grown man. If you can't do it, what message are you sending?"

I faltered, looking down at the table guiltily. No one was giving
any indication of listening to our conversation, but I was sure
they would be. They would be trying to find a loophole. If I got
out of eating, they could copy me and get out of it too.

John knew me too well already, knew exactly what buttons to
push. If I refused to eat, maybe I would be responsible for all these
kids getting worse. But if I stayed and forced myself to eat, maybe
I would help save them. I hated that he was able to do that. I swal-
lowed hard, trying even to the last moment to think of a way out,
but there was none. I sank back reluctantly into my chair, picking
up my fork with a feeling of sickness in the pit of my stomach. My
teeth ached. I wanted to be anywhere else but here.

I tried to focus on anything else, any kind of distraction I could
find, to keep my mind off the food. It wasn't easy. I had nothing
in common with these kids – with their lives, their cultural references, the plans they had for when they got out of here. We were
nothing alike. Even my motivation for starving myself was different from theirs. I doubted any of them were struggling with the
guilt of killing someone.

One by one, the others around me finished their plates, or at least
enough of the food to be excused, and got up to go. It was a rule
here that you stayed at the table until you were done. Part of it
was motivation: if you wanted to retreat to your room, you had
to finish the food you had been given. And there was an element of
shame to it, too. Not wanting to be the last at the table.

Although some saw it as a badge of honour – some like Rachel, who had been staying later and later, still there sometimes long after I had finished and then come back to fetch a drink.

I looked up and blinked; she wasn't there in her usual place. In fact, now that I thought about it, I didn't think I'd seen her at the meal at all.

"What happened to Rachel?" I asked, my voice low, to my nearest neighbour, a shy girl who seemed to hide behind her glasses.

Perhaps predictably, she didn't answer; just shot me a sideways look and cowered in on herself, turning her shoulder as if to block me out.

"She got taken away this morning," Jake, opposite me, spoke up. He must have overheard my question.

"She's been released?" I asked, frowning. It didn't seem right. I wasn't sure that she'd recovered at all. Out of everyone here, she'd probably looked the worst. So thin her bones could snap with a look.

Jakes shook his head, toying with a couple of peas on the tines of his fork. "They took her out in an ambulance. I heard she collapsed."

"She purged her breakfast," the shy girl spoke up, unexpectedly. "I heard her."

I didn't know what to say. I looked down at my plate again, feeling sick for a different reason. Not so long ago, it had been me in that position – and not exactly by choice. Rachel was so young. The damage I had done to myself, to my bones and organs, the damage that I might never recover from – she had done that to herself at such a young age. Even if she survived – and with Rachel, it had to be a big if – she would live with that forever.

It wasn't fair. What had she ever done wrong? She was just a kid. She didn't deserve to be lying there.

I deserved to be lying there. If I could have changed places with her, I would. I wasn't thinking about Ram at that moment, or my parents, or Harry, or anyone else who might have been sad to see me go. I just knew in my bones it was wrong: that an innocent girl was wasting away, and I was getting better, when I had done bad things and never been punished for them.

I took a full scoop of mash and peas and carrot coins and gravy onto my fork, because that was a kind of punishment in itself, and forced mouthful after mouthful down until I felt like I was going to throw it all back up.

5 – RAM

I putter around aimlessly. The house is clean now, but that's all I can bring myself to do. I check the emails of our official business account and find a number of requests from clients, most of which are so old that it's too late to respond to them. I reply to a couple of newer ones, either asking for more details or letting them know that it won't be possible for us to take on their case at this time. The ones with a larger scale, or the ones that would require tech stuff – I can't take those on. Not on my own.

I can't believe that it's already the twentieth of December. 2018 is trickling away from me so quickly, and with it, I feel like I'm losing so many moments that I could have had with Will. Around this time of year, normally we'd be decorating. Buying presents. Will still sends out cards, even though I'm fairly sure he's the only person left under the age of fifty who does. I close my eyes and I can picture him sitting in our apartment in San Francisco, cheerfully writing out messages to all our friends and family back home. I remember how he spent ages searching shops for the most American cards he could find, just to give everyone a kick out of them.

Fuck. It feels like it was so long ago. That was back when I just saw him as a friend – my best friend, the person I trusted above anything else. We could have been rivals when we met. We were both top of the class, both scouted to join the special FBI training programme, both competing for the chance to be an agent. But somewhere along the way, we became a team instead. Every challenge, every training exercise, we worked together – even when we weren't supposed to.

Something in my heart, in my soul, knew from the moment we met that we were two halves of the same whole. I couldn't see exactly how until we first kissed. Until I found out that he's gay, and realised there could be a chance for us. That was when everything changed. Even though I tried to fight it at first, that was when I knew we had to be together – in body as well as in every other way.

And now to have him wrenched away from me – it's like a fucking shot to the chest. Even the bitter image of Kit Anderson that brings to mind, lying on a rooftop in a pool of his own blood, doesn't shake me anymore, not as much as the thought of being without Will. The things we did in the past, the mistakes we made, will always haunt us.

But without him – without him, it's like having not just a ghost on my shoulder, but a black dog too.

There's a box of decorations and a plastic tree in our storage cupboard. I drag them out and set them down in the corner of the living room, and then sit back down on the sofa. I think about getting them out, but I can't. What's the point? What do I have to celebrate if Will's not here?

The intercom buzzes on the wall, making me jump. I'm not expecting anyone. Is this some kind of overzealous client who decided to pay us a home visit? Our address isn't on the website, but if you do a deep enough search, you'd be able to find our company registration details. Since we don't have an office, this is the address on the listing. I think about maybe changing that. If it wasn't so easy to find us, maybe JM Coil might not have been able to hurt us so deeply.

I know he probably would, but anything I can do to increase our security seems like a good move.

I pick up the phone by the intercom, leaning on the wall for support. "Hello?"

"Let me in, Julius!"

I frown. "Alex? ...Did we arrange to meet today?"

"No, we didn't," Alex says, his voice crackling through the line. "Come on, it's cold out here."

I sigh and press the button that unlocks the downstairs door, waiting until I hear his heavy footsteps in the hall outside so that I can let him in. He's wearing a thick overcoat and civilian clothes: a jumper and jeans, not a suit. To my surprise and maybe a little bit of horror, I realise that the jumper has a Fair Isle print with a repeating reindeer motif.

Detective Inspector Alex Heath is wearing a Christmas jumper.

"Alright?" he asks, stomping his feet on our welcome mat and rubbing his hands together. His skin is pale and reddened – I guess he wasn't joking about the cold. I haven't been out for a few days. I wouldn't know.

"Yeah," I lie, looking him up and down for some kind of clue. "What are you doing here?"

"Social visit," Alex grins, taking off his coat and hanging it by the door. "Can I get a hot drink?"

"... Coffee or tea?" I ask, going into some kind of autopilot. I'm still very confused about why he's here. Alex Heath works all hours of the day and fucking night, and he doesn't just drop by unannounced. He's too busy for that. If he has time off, he spends it with his wife, or you have to book him in advance. Like the Ritz.

"Black coffee would be great," Alex says, wandering further into the living room. "It's not very festive in here, is it?"

I reach for a mug in the kitchen, then lean to look at him past the half-wall that is the only division between the kitchen and living room. "Why should it be?"

Alex stares back. "It's five days until Christmas, mate. Four and a half, if you're counting the hours."

"Well, I'm not," I say, dumping coffee granules into the mug with more force than is necessary. "I'm not having Christmas this year."

"Yeah, you are," Alex says. "It doesn't matter whether you're determined to be miserable or not. Christmas still happens."

"Not for me," I mutter. If this is going to be his only line of enquiry, I wish he'd fuck off back to the station.

The intercom goes off again before Alex has a chance to reply, cutting through the apartment. I almost drop the kettle and burn myself with the boiling water I'm pouring over the coffee.

"I'll get that," Alex says cheerily.

"Well, don't let them in if they're chancers," I protest, trying to juggle finishing the coffee I'm making with my desire to go and answer it myself. "People try and get in so they can nick stuff."

"I am actually a member of the Metropolitan Police Force," Alex reminds me drily. "I do know not to let criminals into your building."

I hear him say something quietly into the phone and then put it down, and then he takes his seat again, leaving me to eye him suspiciously as I carry his coffee over.

"Who was it?" I ask. "Did you buzz them in, or not?"

"You'll see," Alex says, with a thoroughly amused expression on his face that I don't like one bit. "Cheers for the coffee."

Then there's a knock at the door, making me even more suspicious. I swear under my breath. "If this is some kind of salesperson..." I say threateningly, but Alex only grins.

I open the door and stop in my tracks. "Asra?" I ask. She's also bundled up in a thick coat, and she's holding a very conspicuously wrapped present in red paper in her hands. There are tiny, glittery snowflakes all over it.

"Hey, Jules," she says, stepping forward. I automatically step back to let her in, even though I have no idea what she's doing here. "Merry Christmas!"

"Jules?" Alex calls from the sofa. "I'm going to have to steal that one."

I scowl at both of them. "No, you won't. What is this? Some kind of ambush?"

"A Christmas ambush," Asra confirms. She's closed the door behind her and pushed the present into my hands, and she's hanging up her coat beside Alex's. Underneath her hijab – bright red today – she's also wearing a cheerful Christmas jumper, bearing a knitted pattern of green holly leaves and red berries on a white background. "We decided you weren't feeling the festive spirit enough."

I look between the two of them incredulously. "How did you even...?"

"Just a tiny abuse of power," Alex says, holding up his finger and thumb very close together. "I got Asra's number from the witness records from that murder near her apartment. Turns out we were both thinking the same thing."

"And what was that?" I scowl, crossing my arms over my chest.

"That you needed cheering up," Alex announces. "We can't be with you on Christmas day, so you'd better consider this our Friends Christmas. By the way – this is yours." He reaches out a hand containing a slim envelope, which I hadn't noticed him bringing in. It must have been in his coat pocket. The envelope is red and features my name in a delicate cursive hand.

"I didn't know you were into calligraphy," I snort, taking it from his hand.

Alex rolls his eyes. "Josie wrote it," he says, then glances at Asra to provide context. "My wife."

"Look, this isn't fair," I say, setting both the card and the present down on the coffee table. "You didn't warn me about this in advance. I haven't got presents for either of you."

"It wouldn't have been a surprise if we'd told you in advance," Asra points out. "Right, where are your Christmas decorations? Or are we going shopping?"

I sigh. "They're over there," I say, gesturing to the cardboard box. "I don't want to put them up. Not this year. Without Will, it's…"

"Will wouldn't want you to be moping away here, having a miserable time," Alex says, getting up and heading over to the box. "Besides, he's not dead, you know. He is coming home eventually."

"I know, but it's not…" I sigh again. I'm not getting into this – not now. "Look, I just don't feel like celebrating this year, alright?"

"That's why we're here," Asra says. She takes both of my hands in hers as Alex starts unpacking the plastic tree. "To get you into the festive spirit. You have so much to celebrate. You faced the kind of villain that I thought only existed in movies – and you survived. You're building a reputation as a premium private detective service, and business has never been better. Not only that, but you've also managed to work on your addiction, and admit your feelings for the man you love. I think that's a pretty big year."

I glance at Alex in protest. "Asra!" I say, wishing she wouldn't go so heavy on the lovey-dovey stuff.

"Don't tell her off on my account," Alex says mildly. "Anyone with a single brain cell and one working eye could tell you're in love with each other. In fact, I don't even think they would need the eye."

"Alright," I say. "Jesus."

"What about food?" Asra asks. "Do you have anything in? I can go and grab us some things to make a little Christmas dinner. What do you think?"

"Fine," I sigh, giving in. It's obvious they aren't going to take no for an answer. "You'd better go. I don't have much in the cupboards."

"Alright." Asra flies into the kitchen anyway, examining cupboards and the fridge, making tutting noises under her breath. "You two get started on the decorations. Do it properly, Julius. I mean it. We'll take pictures so that Will can see them when he gets back."

The suggestion hits me like a blow to the chest. "That would be nice," I admit, struggling to get the words out past the sudden lump in my throat.

"I know, honey, that's why I suggested it," Asra grins, heading for the door again. "I want to see at least the tree up by the time I get back, okay?"

"You'd better help me with these string lights," Alex chuckles. "I think she's serious."

Over the course of the next hours – the decorating of the whole room, Asra's cooking and the delicious smells that start to waft out of the kitchen, and finally the three of us sitting down to eat – I begin to feel better. Just having them here, my two best friends in the world – excluding Will – lifts my spirits. I don't want to tell her, but Asra was right: I did need cheering up.

Both of them must have seen it. I'm lucky to have friends like them. Not that I'm ever going to utter something as mushy as all that.

"What are your traditions, Asra?" Alex asks, throwing down his paper napkin (imprinted with stars and baubles) onto his empty plate. "Do you have Christmas, or not?"

"Yes, we celebrate it," Asra smiles. "When I was growing up, we didn't, at first. It's a Christian holiday, so my parents were against it. But as we grew up I think they wanted us to feel more like we were assimilated here. They're both immigrants, while me and my brother were born here, so they wanted us not to miss out on the things our classmates got to enjoy."

"You just take religion out of it, right?" I ask.

"That's pretty much it. So long as no one's making any references to Jesus, the rest is fine."

I laugh at that. "Yeah, that about suits me as well."

"Josie has to tackle all this kind of stuff at school," Alex says, shaking his head. "They have to call it the winter celebration because there are so many kids from different backgrounds. Can't offend anybody."

"It makes sense," Asra shrugs. "It's nice not to offend people. Although, it can go a little far sometimes, too. I know people are usually a bit reluctant to talk about Christmas with me because they don't know how I'll take it. Some Muslims consider it haram to do anything related with Christmas at all, but I look at it as a way to celebrate with friends and family. It doesn't have to be about one religion or another."

"Hear, hear," Alex says, raising his glass to hers and then draining it. A sparkling non-alcoholic wine, in deference to mine and Asra's sobriety. "You'll be with family on the day?"

"I'm going round to my brother's place," Asra nods. "And you'll be with your wife?"

Alex makes a face. "With my wife's parents. Not the best time of year – I feel like I have to be on my best behaviour instead of getting to relax. But we alternate. Next year will be with my folks."

It sounds nice. I can't help but envy them. "Last time I was with my parents for Christmas was 2009," I say, casually, throwing back the rest of my own drink. I wish it gave me even just a little tiny buzz.

"Nine years ago," Asra says. "You don't talk to them a lot, do you?"

"Not really." I shrug. "I don't get on with my Dad."

"I've wondered about this," Alex says. "You weren't talking to them much back in our training days either, I seem to recall."

"Yeah, well." I take a breath and then get up from the sofa, reaching for my plate to clear it away. "Kind of sucks when everyone knows who your parents are and equates you so closely with them, and you don't even see them much."

"They came to visit you in the hospital, didn't they?" Alex asks.

"Yeah, I guess. I wasn't really awake for it." I laugh to myself. "My mother gave me some old clothes to wear. Including some of my

Dad's merch. Can you believe that? I looked like a fucking prick, walking around in my own Dad's band hoodie."

"Oh, I noticed," Alex chuckles.

"Why didn't you tell me?" I exclaim. "I walked around all fucking day with that on. I didn't see the logo on the back until I took it off. People probably thought I was trying to point out how famous I am or some shit."

"I thought you would take it off immediately if you knew," Alex grins. "You'd just got out of the hospital. You needed to keep warm."

I shake my head in mock outrage. The hoodie was unceremoniously dumped at the bottom of my wardrobe as soon as I took it off.

"Anyway, I'd better head off," Alex says, stretching as he stands up. "Josie will be wanting me back home."

"Me, too," Asra adds. "It's been lovely, though."

"Yeah," I say, looking at the plates that I'm clearing up so I don't have to look either of them in the eye. "Yeah, it was nice, actually. Um. Thanks."

"Any time, Jules," Alex says. I shoot him daggers, and he only laughs in return. "Okay, okay. My real Christmas present to you: I won't call you that again."

"I make no such promise," Asra says. She gets up and kisses me on the cheek, rubbing my shoulder for a brief moment. "Take care of yourself, honey. I'm just a phone call away if you need me."

"I know." I nod my head. "I won't get tempted again. Or if I do, I'll let you know. But I feel better. I really do."

Asra smiles and squeezes my shoulder before letting go. I finish clearing away the dishes and watch them putting on their coats, their shoes, wrapping up for the outside world. I stand awkwardly as they file outside, both of them calling goodbye and me answering, leaning out of the door to watch them disappear down the hall. Something clenches in my chest. I want to call out and tell them to stay. They vanish around the corner and down the stairs, and I shut the door, feeling how empty and alone the house is without them in it.

SIX – WILL

"Damnit," I said out loud, the realisation hitting me full force. I dropped the paintbrush I'd been using all morning, accidentally leaving a splatter of black paint on the table, and rubbed my temple.

"What is it?" Jake asked, looking up from his own work.

We'd been making our Christmas crafts all morning. Claire found me a load of jars that were left over from the kitchen – some that used to hold spices or condiments, some pickled vegetables, some pre-prepared mixes. They were being gathered for recycling, but she brought me the whole box as soon as she heard my idea. I'd been stripping off the labels and soaking the jars to clean them out thoroughly, and now I was painting names on the front in careful lettering. I was doing one for every person in the programme right now. My Christmas gift for everyone.

"I just remembered," I said, groaning. "I got my – uh, my… my roommate a Christmas gift. Now I'm not going to be able to give it to him. It's all wrapped up at home, just waiting."

Jake narrowed his eyes. "Your boyfriend?"

"I didn't say boyfriend," I objected, staring at him.

Jake gave me a knowing look. I hated seventeen-year-olds. They were far too knowing. "You couldn't think of what to call him. So, I'm guessing you at least want him to be your boyfriend."

"Alright, fine," I sighed. "Is that a problem?"

"You'll have to try and let him know," Jake said, putting on a thoughtful expression. "That is definitely going to be a problem. You didn't smuggle in a phone, did you?"

By the way he glossed over the obvious thing I actually meant by my question, I guessed he didn't have a problem with me being gay. Which was a relief. The tension that had just collected in my shoulder blades eased a little. "No, sadly not."

"That's a shame." Jake's own shoulders sagged. "If you did, I would have nicked it off you. Called my girlfriend."

"You have a girlfriend?"

Jake blinks at me. "Thanks for that."

"No," I half-laughed. "I didn't mean anything bad by it. I'm just a bit surprised that… well, that anyone in here has someone."

"You do."

"I just told you I don't," I sighed, and shook my head. "What I have is a reason to get better."

"So do I," Jake said, then ducked his head a little. "Although Claire says I shouldn't think of it like that. She says relying on someone else as a reason to get better can be dangerous. Like, if they decide they don't want to be with you anymore."

The thought sent a spike of panic into my gut. He wouldn't, would he?

I would just have to do something to make sure that I stayed top of his mind – that he didn't forget me while I was away. The thought of him going out and sleeping around again made me sick to my stomach, and not just because I was worried about his health. I wanted him to wait for me. It was selfish, but I wanted him to be there when I got out. For that closeness we had only just discovered to not have evaporated in my absence.

"We'll just have to find a way to get the word out," I said, not wanting to dwell on that possibility anymore. "You can help me. We'll find a way to contact your girlfriend, too."

"But how?" Jake asked, wrinkling up his nose. "You know outside contact isn't allowed. The only phone I've seen in the whole place is on Claire's desk. I don't even think they let staff bring their mobiles in."

I shook my head. "In this day and age? Even if they're banned from bringing them in, someone will. The staff have lockers for their stuff during the day, right?"

"Yeah, in the room next to Claire's office," Jake confirmed. "I've seen them going in and out in the mornings when I can't sleep."

I nodded slowly. "Then we're just going to have to find a way to get to them. We need to know who brings in a phone, get into that room, and also get into the locker."

"That sounds impossible. We're not master thieves in a spy film," Jake scoffed.

I grinned at him. "You haven't known me very long, have you?" I asked, enjoying his confused and wide-eyed expression in response.

7 – RAM

I take a deep breath and enter the login details, wishing I could stay in the dark for longer. I can't, of course. I have to step up and be an adult at some point here.

Will has always been the one who deals with the grown-up shit. Making sure the bills get paid, keeping track of our finances, ordering the grocery shopping. I just went out and partied and he took care of everything. Well, now I'm paying for it, because I'm finding out all of the things that I have no idea how to deal with.

The balance in our joint account flashes in front of my eyes, making me groan and cover my face. Since we were kidnapped by JM Coil, neither of us have been working, quite obviously. Will has probably still been earning some royalties from his books, but they go into his personal account, and I can't access that.

And my personal account is currently gathering dust and cobwebs, and literally fuck all else.

Fucking hell. We used to have so much money in this account. JM Coil paid us, not once but twice. First as a reward for solving the Highgate Strangler case, which it turned out he was orchestrating from behind the scenes specifically to challenge us – which, looking back, makes a lot of our lucky discoveries seem like anything but. Then as a way to drive a wedge of suspicion between us through a mystery payment. The good news is that we had already spent a large portion of the Highgate Strangler money on rent and bills and food. The bad news is that JM Coil, or whoever might have been acting on his behalf, took back the second payment and what he could recover of the first as soon as he had us in captivity.

Even if he hadn't, I guess it's possible that the police would have put a hold on the money while they investigated. We wouldn't have been much better off. But this – this is bad. All we had left was the profits from a few recent cases, and they didn't add up to much.

"Alright, Ram," I say out loud, trying to give myself some form of motivation. "You're going to have to deal with this."

Yep. Deal with it. But how the fuck am I going to do that?

A pang hits my chest, a physical pain. I want two things. I want a drink so that I don't have to think about how bad this could be, how I could end up losing the apartment before Will gets out of rehab, leaving him with no home to come back to. And I want Will, here by my side, helping me deal with this.

Everything is always so much easier with him around. Even before I realised how I feel about him, he made everything better. He's patient and organised and logical, everything I'm not. He doesn't hate numbers like I do. He's even smart enough to have a second revenue stream lined up, while I just... what? Do absolutely everything half-arsed until I'm left with nothing?

Fuck. I can't think like that right now, even if it might be justified. I need to focus, to think.

I open a few websites things, that might help. I need to think like Will would, and that means going digital. I search Facebook groups and pages, Craigslist, Twitter hashtags, online message boards, local police websites. By the end of the morning, I have a small list: missing persons, people reporting thefts that haven't yet been solved, even an arson. Somewhere in here, there has to be someone with the means and the urgency to hire a private detective.

I take a deep breath, wishing for the nine hundredth time this month that Will was here with me, and pick up my phone to make a call.

EIGHT – WILL

"What are you going to write?" Jake asked, staring down at his notebook with a frown.

"I don't know yet," I sighed. It seemed like something more carefully selected was needed than a simple 'hey, I got you a present'. Whether it was the fact that we couldn't see each other for so long or the fact that we were having to be covert about getting the message through, it felt like I had to write something more momentous.

"Do girls really like the totally mushy stuff, or is that just movies?" Jake asked.

"Why are you asking me?" I snorted. "I have no idea."

Jake shrugged. "Good point. I'm just stuck. I don't want to scare her off."

"Just write something from the heart," I said. "Anyone would like that."

"I hope so." Jake stuck his tongue out between his lips, concentrating hard, as he put pen to paper. After a few seconds, he sighed and scribbled out whatever he had been writing. "This is hard."

"Just write a first draft," I encouraged him. "We'll edit it later."

"We?" Jake looked hopeful. "Will you help me?"

"Only if you help me," I smiled.

I looked down at my own blank page, the words still refusing to come. What could you say in a situation like this? Everything was so uncertain. The last time I'd seen Ram, we'd both been in hospital, recovering from what was done to us. If the trauma and the nightmares followed him like they followed me, I had no idea what kind of mental state he would be in. I had the benefit of mandated therapy sessions in here. He was on his own.

And then there was the question of us – if there was an us. All the things we thought we'd done to each other, the imagined hurts, they were all just creations of Coil. None of it was real. We'd kissed, and then we'd thought we might die together, and of course, things had been very strange and intense. I could still feel that kiss if I closed my eyes and concentrated. I could remember the feeling of his hands on my hips, pulling me closer, before all of this. I could remember the heat and the slick of us, the single time we had been together. My first.

But all of that was in the past, and I had no idea what the future held for us. What could I write? Some madcap declaration of love? And what if he'd already moved on out there? Or I could get it wrong in the other direction – send him something simple and plain, no word of love at all, and leave him disappointed if he was hoping for more.

It was so hard to know what to do. Jake was right. This was a guessing game, the kind of game that people must have agonised over back in the days when writing a letter was your only option. When seeing the one you loved meant several days riding in a carriage, and you had to be invited first, and even then have a chaperone. God, that must have been awful.

I tried to imagine how it might have been to be in this place, this position, without having known his touch already. It would have been so much worse. I was glad we managed to have that one night together, even if it was so long ago now, and even if at the time we tried to pretend it meant nothing. I remember how I felt hot tears gathering inside my eyes while he bent over me, his face buried in my hair so he couldn't see, wondering if it would be the only time.

I hoped desperately that it wouldn't be the only time.

"I'm going to make it into a game," I said, finally settling on something that could work. "Like a scavenger hunt."

"What, to help him find the present you've hidden?" Jake asked. "But you can only risk getting one message out. What if you do the first one and then can't get access to the phone again?"

"You're right." I chewed my lip. "A riddle, then. Just a few lines."

"That sounds amazing," Jake said, his eyes lighting up. "You're good at this. He's totally going to love you after he sees that, even if he doesn't already. I wish I had something to direct Becca to."

"Let me see what you've got so far," I said, holding out my hand for his notebook. I'd make good on my promise to help him. I didn't want him to feel like his message wasn't going to be as good as mine.

We spent hours poring over each word of our messages, crafting them carefully, deliberating each syllable like it was poetry. In the end, we were satisfied: Jake with a heartfelt message that he felt sure would win Becca over if she had drifted away, and me with a riddle. I looked it over one last time as John appeared to tell us all that craft time was over and to head back to our rooms, sure I had done as much as I could to make it perfect.

I sleep and dream of time with you
This Christmas there's much I can't do
But know me, seek, and you will find
That you rest still inside my mind

9 – RAM

"For God's sake." I run my hands over my face, aware that talking to myself out loud is probably a bad indication of my level of coping. I wipe sweat from my forehead with the back of my arm, feeling how my hair is plastered down to it. The sheets of the bed around me are soaked through.

I can't go on like this. I get up wearily, heading on stumbling, still sleepy feet towards the shower to rinse myself off with cold water. It's the only thing that will dispel the lingering images of the nightmare: Will, wasted away almost to a skeleton, breathing shakily in my arms in a cold and dark cell until the breathing finally stops.

I check the clock as I stumble back out of the shower: four in the morning. Just fucking perfect. But I'm awake now. I can't bear going back to sleep, in case the dream comes back again. I strip the sheets off the bed, remake it with clean ones, and then sit down, wondering what to do for the next three and a half hours before I can start calling people.

The cases I tried to pursue yesterday all turned out to be dead ends. Some of them had already been solved, and others were from clients who didn't have enough budget to afford me. Not even at half price. I thought about helping them anyway – it's always been the love of the challenge, the puzzle, more than the money for me – but that wouldn't get me closer to being able to pay the bills.

I can't just give up. It's not an option. I can't let us lose the apartment before Will comes home. So, what am I going to do?

There is one possibility – one that I don't want to think about yet.

A Hail Mary. But I haven't got to that point, not until I've tried absolutely everything I can. I've already checked with Alex, and he doesn't have anything I could come in on. But that doesn't mean there isn't work out there. I just have to look a bit harder for it.

I check our emails one more time, see another message – from one of the queries we'd had before. A woman looking for a stolen necklace, who regrets to inform me that she's already found someone else. She was the last one I was waiting to hear back from – the others had all moved on to other solutions, too. Fuck. I wasn't on the ball – wasn't paying enough attention. I missed out on so many chances. I've let Will down.

I close my eyes for a moment. I can't let this happen. I have to find a way to keep us here.

I spend the rest of the morning looking up lists, trying to find viable contact details. And when eight in the morning ticks around, I start making calls.

"Hello, you've reached PCI Studio. How can I help?"

"Hi, I'm just getting in touch as I'm a private detective. I wanted to let you guys know about our services and what we can offer you in terms of corporate solutions," I say, starting in on a carefully rehearsed spiel. "We're able to conduct in-house investigations into matters of fraud, NDA follow-up, theft of company property, surveillance of employees or rival companies, and any other matters that you feel could benefit from our skills. We're available right now and over the next week as a matter of priority."

"Yeah, sorry, we're not really looking for anything like that right now," the receptionist, or business owner, or whoever the fuck I've managed to get in touch with, says. "It's right before Christmas, you know? Most of our staff have already gone on leave, and I don't think it's something we'd need anyway."

"Right," I say, disheartened. "Well, if you could keep our details on file..."

"Sure," she says. "Thanks for the call. Bye-bye now."

Before I can do anything else, she puts the phone down. I sigh. I didn't even manage to tell her the name of our business.

I dial another number from my list, and another. All of them have their own reasons: some of them don't want to engage in that kind of practise at all and would rather contact the police if they needed to. Some of them tell me they don't have the budget, or that the people who make those decisions have already left for their Christmas break. Others tell me they'll keep us in mind, though I don't hold out much hope. I work my way down all of the lists I had managed to put together, and still nothing.

I don't know what to do. It seems like the Julius Rakktersen charm, the one tool I normally rely on, is letting me down. Maybe it's because I'm talking over the phone and not in person. Maybe it's just that no one can be bothered with business right now, with Christmas right around the corner. Then again, maybe there's just no work out there, because the universe seems to be determined to fuck me over.

First, it sics a deranged psychopath on us and puts us in hospital. Then it takes Will away from me and keeps him away for Christmas. And now there's no money, and no work either. Just fucking great.

I bury my head in my hands and try not to scream so loudly the neighbours will call the police.

TEN – WILL

I sat quietly in the craft room while everyone else finished their Christmas gifts. A cardboard box full of neatly painted mason jars sat on the desk in my room; it turned out I was great at crafting fast when I had some motivation to get it done early, so I could focus on other things.

I gave Jake a meaningful look across the room, and he returned it. He was still pretending to finish off his gifts – little origami shapes he was making based on the instructions on a book that was in the small library here – even though he, too, had finished them yesterday so we could work on our mutual project.

Unfortunately for me, Claire had pretty quickly noticed that I wasn't doing anything. I'd shown her my finished work, hoping she would let me just sit quietly and do my own thing, but no such luck. She'd told me I should find something else to work on, so I'd asked for some supervised computer time.

I was sure she regretted it when she saw what I was searching for. We weren't allowed unsupervised access in case we tried to contact people from home, or go on social media, or look at things that could be triggering. What I was looking for was none of those things. In fact, I was looking at cold cases – unsolved murders that I could sink my teeth into. It wasn't likely that I was going to get anywhere with solving them, but it would at least be a good distraction.

I looked at cases like this as training. Not just trying to hone my mind, but also seeing where the original investigation went wrong. Sometimes, leads were lost that could never be found again. That's why I found myself sitting in the craft room surrounded by print-outs of all the cold cases I could find from the last forty years in the London area, studying them one by one.

And probably also why Claire had looked a bit green by the time I was finished with my computer time.

"Are you ready?" Jake muttered, moving closer to me and sitting down at the next table.

I nodded, trying not to look at him, but instead glancing up to make sure that Claire wasn't watching us. "As soon as she takes a break."

We'd already had some luck first thing this morning: Jake had been loitering in the hall, just around the corner from the staff room, watching everyone come in for their shifts. That was how he'd seen John slip a phone out from his pocket and into the side of a rucksack that he was carrying with him. He then left the staff room without it, meaning that it was still inside.

The next problem we had to solve was the key, which, as far as we knew, was inside John's pocket now. He was wearing a fleece jacket against the cold, one side of which hung suspiciously straight as if there was a weight holding it down.

I picked up another printout and started reading it. This one looked like the most interesting case yet: the Thames Valley Stalker, a suspected serial killer who had taken victims back in the eighties. One day the killings had just stopped, even though no one had ever been apprehended for the crimes. The prevailing theory was that the person responsible had been caught for something else and put in prison, and remained there to this day.

But there wasn't a confirmed suspect, and all of the guesses I read as to the perpetrator were slightly off. No one could seem to agree on who might have done it. All of which made for some very interesting prospects as far as research was concerned.

I felt Jake's elbow nudge my ribs painfully, yanking my attention from the paper in my hand. He was right: Claire had slipped out of the room, perhaps to go to the toilet. Now was our chance.

"You get John," I whispered. "I'll go see if the coast is clear."

Jake gave me a determined nod and headed to the other side of the room, where John was sitting deep in conversation with one of the younger members of the programme. I didn't stop to watch how Jake would get the keys – or if he would be successful. I had my own part of the plan to play, and I had to trust him to get it done. It was an unfamiliar feeling, trusting anyone but Ram.

I headed quickly into the hall and glanced around, seeing no one. It was a short walk around the corner to where, as I'd hoped, the staff room was empty. Everyone was working throughout the centre, and the lockers were abandoned.

And, I saw, we'd had another stroke of luck, too.

"I couldn't get the keys," Jake said, bursting into the room breathlessly. "He saw me coming up behind him and asked what I wanted."

"It doesn't matter," I grinned. "Look."

John's backpack was sitting on top of the lockers, unattended. It was clearly too large to fit inside the spaces, so John had just dumped it up there.

Jake laughed with glee and quickly reached up to grab it. That was another thing that annoyed me: at seventeen, and even weighing about as much as a wet chihuahua, Jake was also already much taller than me.

"Here," he said, fishing the phone out of the pocket. "Have you got the paper?"

"Right here," I said. I took the phone and started typing as fast as I could – first the message to his girlfriend, along with the number he had written down for her. We agreed that I would type them out as I had the quickest fingers, but I felt duty-bound to send his first. After all, if we got caught and I'd only managed to send my own message…

Jake stood at the doorway, keeping it propped open, watching for anyone who might be coming. If he saw someone, I would have to put the phone back fast, or there wouldn't be an opportunity to use it again. They'd catch on and John would lock it away. I shoved Jake's paper back into my pocket as the message sent and pulled out my own, typing everything faithfully word for word. After spending so much time on crafting the message, the last thing I wanted was to send it incorrectly.

I checked every word twice, then hit the send button, my hands shaking. It was done.

Then it hit me, and I swore under my breath.

"What?" Jake muttered.

"I've just sent him a creepy message from an unknown number," I muttered. "That's not romantic. That's going to freak him out." I passed a hand over my face quickly, trying to think.

"Just tell him it's from you," Jake hissed urgently, looking at me for a moment before glancing back over his shoulder. "Come on, hurry up and put it back!"

"Hold on," I muttered.

> I sleep and dream of time with you
> This Christmas there's much I can't do
> But know me, seek, and you will find
> That you rest still inside my mind

This is Will, by the way. Happy hunting!

It's a riddle. If that wasn't clear. I bought you a present.

Anyway, happy Christmas

"Will, stop," Jake hissed in my direction, his face full of panic. I fumbled with the phone and dropped it just as I hit send on the last message, still unfinished. After all that time I'd spent on carefully planning what to say, and I'd still managed to mess it up and sound like an idiot.

I grabbed the phone up off the floor again, reaching for the backpack to put it away –

"So, would you like to explain what you're doing in here?"

I looked up guiltily. There was no way to hide anymore – Claire was looking right at me, right at the phone in my hand.

"Sorry, mate," Jake said, looking downcast. I understood why. We were in trouble now – and he hadn't been able to prevent Claire from seeing what I was doing.

Our pipeline to the outside world was gone. I only hoped that Ram could understand my riddle and that he didn't think I was a complete idiot from what I'd written – because I wasn't going to be getting any kind of contact privileges for the rest of my time here.

11 – RAM

I stare at my phone, my heart racing in my chest. It pounds so hard it hurts, sending thuds through my ribcage.

Is this really a message from him?

I don't know the number, so I guess he must have borrowed a phone. I thought that wasn't allowed. I think about writing something back – my fingers fly to the keyboard at the bottom of the screen – but then I hesitate. If it's a stranger's phone, I don't know if I want to write something that others will read. And it seems pretty hurried.

And what would I even say?

I overthink it for so long that I realise I've been just sitting and staring at the message, and by now, Will has almost certainly handed the phone back. I don't want to ruin things, so I just shake my head to clear it and read the riddle again. I won't message back – but I will find this present he's left for me.

A present… my heart lifts in my chest again. If there's a present somewhere here for me, does that mean he thought about it even before he went away? Before Coil, before he stayed with Harry, before we argued? Just how early did he buy this present? I think of him seeing something for me back in August or something and smile, the thought burning through me like the warmth of whiskey.

Alright – but what does it even mean? I read the riddle through carefully, frowning. Something about him dreaming of me – well, that's nice, I guess. So long as it isn't the kind of dreams I've been having. But as for the location of this present – the clue seems to be in the lines '*know me, seek, and you will find – that you rest still inside my mind*'.

Well, what the fuck does that mean?

I growl to myself, frustrated. The whole riddle seems to just repeat itself – that he's thinking about me. Which I love, but, what? How does that help me figure out where to search? Does he just think that if I 'know' him well enough, I'll know where to look?

Besides, I tore this house apart already, looking for cameras. What could I possibly have missed?

I run a hand through my hair, trying to think. Know him – like in the biblical sense, maybe? Right here on the sofa was where we first fucked. I mean, I wouldn't expect Will to be so bold as to reference it right out, but I guess... it's a start? I pull the cushions off the sofa and hunt around beneath it, but there doesn't seem to be anything here.

We woke up in bed together – my bed. Maybe that's what he means. After all, we did take it to the bedroom. Alright, fine – I take my bed apart too, even lifting the mattress because I don't know what I'm looking for. It could be as slim as an envelope, right?

But there's nothing here. I stop again and turn in circles, trying to think, getting more frustrated by the moment. Know him – I thought I did know him. But I can't think what the fuck he means. Is there a special place, somewhere really meaningful to him? I would have guessed the sofa as that's where he spends most of his time, but I already looked there.

Know him... I... do I even know him at all?

I sink down onto my haphazardly thrown-together bed, closing my eyes and sliding my hands over my face. Why can't I figure out what he means? I think about that night, the night we were in here together, when it was like my wildest fantasy come true. I never told him that. I never told him how hot it was, him coming onto me like that. The way he asked me to take him, gave in to my every move and command, trusted me to make it good for him.

I can still see him. I feel like it might be one of those memories that you never forget, not even when you're in a nursing home and can't remember your kids' names. His beautiful face, all angles, contorted with pleasure as he opened up under me. His shiny jet-black hair cast back against the pillow, my pillow, his smooth and soft body under my hands. The way I could fit my hands around his waist and almost touch my fingers together, wondering if I was going to break him – the only thing I would ever want to change.

My straight best friend, or so I had thought, gasping for me in my bed. I couldn't believe how lucky I was then. And now, to think I might have a chance to have him there every night – if I can only hold on and wait for him to come home.

God, it hurt so much when he pretended afterwards like it didn't mean anything. I can't go through that again. When he comes home, we have to make this work. We have to try.

If he won't, I don't know how I'm ever going to get over him.

TWELVE – WILL

"Will, you know why you're here," Claire said.

I didn't look up from where I was slumped in a chair in front of her. Maybe playing the sullen teenager was a predictable move, one that wasn't going to earn me many points, but I didn't have anything else in the arsenal. I'd been caught fair and square. I didn't know what she was planning to do. Lock me in my room? Take away my already slim privileges? Kick me out of the programme?

As much as I wanted to leave and see Ram, I knew that was a bad idea. I would have to find somewhere else – and at Christmas, too. Not a high chance of success. I was hopeful that maybe she would just yell at me for a while and send me to my room.

Claire sighed. "I expected this kind of behaviour from the younger residents," she said. "But, honestly, Will, I'm surprised. You're not a lovesick teenager trying to contact a crush. I know it can be hard at this time of year, but we wanted to look to you to set an example."

"Aren't I?" I asked, raising my eyes to meet hers. I was angry, not just at the fact that I was trapped here thanks to my own stupidity but also because she was refusing to give me the confrontation I wanted. It was like being back home again. The Ambassador wasn't one to yell. He would just quietly lecture you on how disappointed he was.

"Aren't you...?" Claire's expression was blank.

"A lovesick teenager." I gave a short, sharp laugh. "I've never been in a relationship, and this is only my second time dealing with a – a crush, if you want to call it that. So, I probably am on about that level, actually."

Claire refolded her arms on top of the notebook in her lap, looking at me keenly. "You've been struggling with things for a very long time, Will, haven't you?" she asked. "You haven't opened up much in your therapy sessions, and you don't like to talk in the group. The thing is, this process is a two-way street. The more you give us, the better we're able to help you. The better you can help yourself."

I shrugged. "I don't like talking about myself."

Claire was choosing her words carefully, talking slowly. "Those who don't like to talk about themselves are usually the ones who could benefit the most from doing so. Can you tell me when your eating disorder started? Is it something you've had for a long time, or was it sparked by a trigger event?"

"A bit of both." I studied my own hand, the thinness of my fingers, which I had always thought were elegant. I liked my hands. I liked that Ram could wrap his hand around my wrist, his finger and thumb easily overlapping. I liked that I was delicate. Why did I have to give that up?

"Then let's talk about earlier in your life," Claire said. "Have you always felt like you were different from the people around you?"

I scoffed. "Yes. Look at me. I'm not the same as the people I grew up with. No one could deny that."

"And in other ways as well?" Claire prompted.

I looked down again. I was expecting a dressing down, not an impromptu therapy session. But it's not like I could just get up and walk out of here and refuse to talk. I needed this programme. I needed to get healthy so I could go back to him. "I didn't understand my sexuality for a long time," I said, at length. "I'm still not sure I do."

"That's something I'd like to explore in depth with you in another session," Claire said. "But, for now, I'd like to take the point that you felt different in many ways from your peers. That must have been isolating."

I scratched the back of my head. For some reason, my scalp was itching. "I suppose it was."

"Did you ever commit any form of self-harm before you started to restrict your eating habits?" Claire asked. "You told me the restriction started last year – December 2017."

"It did," I nodded. "But I guess I played with it before that. Not allowing myself to have treats when I felt I'd done something wrong. Messed up. I..."

"Yes?"

I hesitated, but Claire's eyes were boring into me. "I felt like I had to measure up. I was adopted. My parents were... my father was an important man. Still is, I suppose, even though he's retired now. I felt I had to be worthy of the sacrifice they made in taking me on. I had to be less of a burden."

Claire leaned forward keenly. "Do you still feel that way? That you have to be worthy of your friends, your family, your loved ones?"

I shrugged helplessly. "Yes."

"And do you feel that you are worthy? Right at this moment?"

"No."

Claire left a pause, allowed that information to sink in. "Will, I want to tell you something, and I know that it might not be something that you accept just yet. But we don't love people because we judge them to be worthy or unworthy. If my husband makes a mistake, I don't love him less. And I wouldn't love him more if he was perfect. You told me about your business partner – the man you live with."

"Ram." I breathed the word, through a raw throat.

"You told me that he's an alcoholic, in recovery now," Claire said. "Did you value him less when he was drinking?"

"No," I said. "I was upset with him. Frustrated. I wanted him to take better care of himself."

"So, how do you think he feels about you?" Claire asked. "No matter who you are or how well you fit in, or what you've done in the past, you don't have to measure yourself constantly against a benchmark or punish yourself when you perceive that you've failed. Ram wants you to take better care of yourself. He may be upset or frustrated with you, but he wouldn't want you to damage yourself because of that."

"That's not everything," I said, my throat impossibly thick now. "It's not the whole story. There was – something..."

"Your trigger point." Claire stated it rather than asking.

"I did something," I said, swallowing. I averted my eyes from hers, down at the floor. "Something bad."

"Can you tell me about it?"

"No." I didn't miss a single beat. There was never any chance that I would be able to talk about what we had done to anyone. Not a priest, not a lawyer, not a doctor, not a therapist. No one. The only people who could ever know were me and Ram. It was the only way to be safe.

Claire bit her lip momentarily. "Will, sometimes the things we carry around with us are not as bad as they seem. If you could open up to me..."

"No," I cut her off, again. A twisted smile contorted my lips. "Trust me. I did just about the worst thing someone could do. Talking about it won't make it better. It would just make you... it would make you face a legal dilemma. Let's leave it at that."

Claire drew in a sharp breath. "Alright." She nodded, gathering herself for a moment before carrying on. "Even so. I don't believe there's anything so bad that you can't redeem yourself from it. It's about how you live your life from that moment, not what you did before."

"And that's how I've been living," I told her, desperate now. "Repenting. Punishing myself. Allowing myself only as much as I needed to live. If I hadn't been locked in that room without food, I could have carried on just as I was. I was staying alive."

"But you weren't staying healthy, Will," she interrupted. "I think you need to face that. As much as you may have been surviving until that point, you were on a downhill tumble. Sooner or later, you would have been hospitalised either way. You've done damage to your body that can't be recovered. And if you go back into that damaging cycle, I'm afraid that you'll die."

I met her proclamation with silence. It wasn't like I hadn't heard it before. Still, it made me surly, rather than changing my ways. I didn't know what I was supposed to take from that. No matter what warnings I was given, I still did what I did. I still needed to make up for that, however I could. It went beyond what she was talking about before – beyond worthiness. It was about redemption. Something I didn't ever truly believe I could achieve – but that shouldn't have stopped me from trying to find it.

"Look," she said. "There's more work we can do together, but I need you to be fully committed to this programme. Do you understand? We want you to recover, to go out and live a healthy, normal life. To not be trapped by these feelings anymore. But in order to stay here, you need to follow the rules – and Jake does too. We don't want to have to have either of you leave us before your recovery is complete."

A spike of guilt hit me like a needle in the chest. "I messed up his recovery."

Claire paused, assessing me. "Does that make you feel guilty?"

"Yes." I shook my head at her in disbelief. How could she even ask? "Of course, it does."

"And how does that affect you?" Claire asked. "What do you do when you feel like this?"

"I... stop eating," I told her, even though I knew it would make them watch me closely at the next meals. I felt like I couldn't lie to her just then. She was tapping into something deep inside me that made me want to spill everything. Everything but that which wasn't only mine to tell.

"Instead of doing that, I want you to try something else for me," Claire said. "We're going to do a couple of new techniques, alright?"

I nodded mutely. Even if I didn't believe she could help me – didn't believe that I was worthy of being helped – I could go along with the pretence. Perform the moves.

"The first thing I want you to do is an affirmation. With an affirmation, we're telling ourselves a positive story, instead of the negative ones we always told ourselves in the past. If you feel guilty, or unworthy, or less than, or different, I want you to repeat this affirmation – either in your head, or out loud. And you can practice this at other times, too. When you get up in the morning is a good time. I want you to say it after me, ready? Say, I am a good person who deserves to be loved and forgiven."

I stared at her.

There was no way.

No way I could ever say anything like that.

"Will," Claire said gently. "Please. Even if you don't believe the words, I want you to say them. Do it for me just once, at least."

I shook my head, clenching my fists into balls. My knuckles felt like they were going to pop.

Claire leaned forward and gently took my hands, her cool fingers laying over the strain of the joints. "I am a good person who deserves to be loved and forgiven."

I couldn't turn away from her. I felt a tear rolling down my cheek. I started with a cracking voice, feeling raw and bleeding inside, like I was blaspheming against a higher power, inviting demons to take up residence in my chest. "I am a g-... A good person."

"Who..."

"Who deserves to be lo-. I can't."

"You can, Will. All the way through. I am a good person who deserves to be loved and forgiven."

"I am a..." I took a breath, closed my eyes, and forced it out. "I am a *good person who deserves to be loved and forgiven.*"

"Well done." Claire drew back from me, leaving a moment's silence. "Keep your eyes closed for a moment, Will. Try and feel the environment around you. Feel the ground under your feet. The fabric of the chair under your hands. Become aware of each of your senses in turn. Listen to my voice – listen to the birds outside. Take a deep breath and smell the coffee on my desk. Slowly now, open your eyes and let your sight come back. That's it."

I did everything she told me to do, slowly, carefully, sending out my senses one by one. A feeling of calm took over for just a moment before I opened my eyes and the real world came flooding back. Still, I found that I didn't want to run to the bathroom quite so badly, didn't want to force myself to purge the lunch I'd eaten. Not that I could manage it here without getting caught. But the urge was dying away.

"You're doing really well, Will," Claire said with a smile. "We'll try this again in our next session. Try and ground yourself whenever these feelings come over you, and practice the affirmation if you can. I think you've just made a real breakthrough."

I got up and headed for the door, feeling strangely both there and not there, wondering whether I really was making progress or I was just a really convincing fraud.

13 – RAM

I sit on the sofa, feeling Will's absence in the space next to me more keenly than ever. If he was here, maybe doing this would be bearable.

If he was here, I wouldn't need to do it at all.

I stare down at the phone in my hand. This is it – I have to do it. I don't have a choice anymore. No one is hiring, and I doubt they will be until well after the New Year, and even then who knows how long it will take for me to bring in enough work to cover all of the bills.

I need help, and I need it now.

I think about calling him, but my nerve fails me. I can't talk to him on the phone. Over these years, his voice has become a trigger for me – it riles me up, gets me angry, makes me say things I shouldn't. That won't work when I'm begging him for help. I need to do this in a calm way. I need to handle myself.

I start the message twenty or thirty times, each time deleting it and starting again. Bile rises up in my throat. I think about the last time I asked him for anything – the very last time I ever thought I was going to ask for his help. I vowed to myself then that I would never need him again. He let me down. But I can't let my pride stand in the way. This isn't just for me – it's for Will. It's for our home, together. And if we don't have a home together, if we don't have a business, if we both have to get jobs somewhere else – I don't know if we'll manage to have a future together.

And a future without Will is one that I'm just not interested in.

I finally clench my jaw and hold my nerve for long enough to hit send. It feels like an electric spark hits my thumb as I touch the button, and even as soon as it's gone, I want to claw the message back, to somehow delete it before he sees it. But I know that's not possible. It's done. It's out there – no chance to change it now.

> Hey, Dad. I need your help. Will's still sick and we can't pay for apartment. Will pay you back ASAP. Please.

I stare at the message on the screen for a long time, tension thrumming through my shoulders and back. I clench every muscle in my body when the indicator changes all of a sudden, without warning: a small tick appearing next to the text, indicating that the message has been read. He's seen it.

I wait a long time for him to reply. To call me. I feel sick to my stomach waiting. I'm going to have to talk to him now. Years avoiding this motherfucker, and now I'm going to have to talk to him because Will needs it. I have to stay strong.

But there's no call. No message. I'm still waiting when an email notification comes through. I open it and read, barely believing what I see: it's a bank transfer alert. A payment has just come in.

I read the balance screen seven times and I still don't believe it. Not just enough to cover a month's rent, like I had expected. Far more. Six months' worth, plus enough to cover utilities and bills for the same period, with some left over. I can't tell whether my father has lost touch with reality enough to have no idea how much our apartment costs, or whether he's just being generous.

And still, there was no message. No indication of how long he was giving me to pay it back. No questions about how Will was doing – how I was doing, for that matter. Last time he'd seen me, I'd been asleep in a hospital bed. Or so I assumed. By the time I woke up only my Mum was around, and she said he'd been and gone. Maybe she was just telling me that to make me feel better.

Fuck, and he sent me the money. Now what am I supposed to feel?

I've got by for years without having to talk to that fucker. I've spoken to Mum plenty, I've put up with him grudgingly when she made me visit before we went to San Francisco. I saw her once this whole year, after getting back to London, and that was for dinner in a Chinatown restaurant – my treat, to say hello again and to avoid having to go back to their home. Of course, the whole experience was somewhat ruined by the paparazzi that still follow her around whenever she ventures out of the countryside.

There were plenty of headlines about me and them when I was in hospital, too. I caught a few of them. Lurid stories about how this rocker and model's son was kidnapped and tortured. Rags that aren't worth the paper they're printed on trying to dig into my personal life, bringing up old images from the days when I was too drunk to care who photographed me vomiting in the street. Even Will's past was dredged up – images of his father shaking hands with Prince Charles, an old school photograph. I hoped at the time that he wouldn't see them, and I've never shown them to him. With luck, no one ever will.

All part and parcel of having famous parents. And it always comes back to the same thing: how unfair it is that I still get tarred with their brush, still get that unwanted attention, when I don't even know who they are. And him – Matthias. How can I even call him a father when we haven't spoken properly in years, when he spent my whole childhood drugged out of his mind and too busy touring to even notice me?

Fuck. I rub my hands over my eyes, a gesture that is starting to feel way too habitual. I didn't need to dredge any of this up again, not when I'm supposed to be focusing on my recovery. But I need the cash. Even if I don't really want it to be from him, there aren't a whole lot of other avenues open to me.

I lay back on the sofa, propping my head against one of the arms, and try to find some way to distract myself. It's Christmas Eve;

normally I would be with Will, helping him prepare some kind of festive food for tonight, going out and getting him a last-minute present. This year would have to be the one year in my whole life that I've actually remembered ahead of time, wouldn't it? The one time I can't actually give it to him.

I already know Alex and Asra are going to be busy tomorrow. I start scrolling through my contacts list, feeling unbearably lonely. I've literally never spent Christmas Day alone. The whole of my adult life, Will's been there, right from our first year in training together. Five Christmases in a row. Enough that I already don't really know what to do with myself without him here.

Before that, I would spend time with friends. I was at uni, and there were always more than enough people in halls or on my course who didn't leave. Some of them were international students who couldn't spend the plane fare. Others were like me: they just didn't want to go back. We did what we could. Made the most of things.

So, I look through my contacts list, trying to find someone like me. Someone who won't want to be home.

Most of the listings are just a first name: men I met through Grndr or just in bars, whose contact details I took only to ignore their calls and messages from then on. Some of them aren't even names – just descriptions. I start deleting the ones I can't even remember, and some of the ones that I do and wouldn't ever want to come across again. By the time I'm done, my contacts list has been reduced to a fifth of its previous size. And I'm still none the wiser on who I could possibly call to spend time with tomorrow.

Well, there is one name that I noticed on the way through. A name I really don't think I should be turning to. But right now, I don't know if I have any other option.

I think about spending tomorrow without Will and my stomach drops. Any kind of distraction would be better than nothing. Even if it's not someone I ever thought I would be talking to again, at least we both care about Will. Maybe he can even sympathise.

> Harry, it's Julius. Do you have plans for tomorrow?

I hit send with my heart in my mouth, wondering what exactly has become of me. Once upon a time, I would never have dreamed of reaching out to someone like Harry. Being vulnerable with him, allowing him the chance to reject me. I guess once upon a time, I wasn't so in love with Will that I feel it like a physical ache in my chest. And if it did hurt, I had him with me to ease the pain.

I don't have to wait long for the reply. I try to picture Harry getting my message, what his reaction might have been, but I can't see it. He's a blank to me. I never really got to know him – not like Will has.

> Yeah, I'm already with my family for the holidays. Why, were you planning something for Will?

Something for Will. That's a good enough excuse. I can use that.

> Never mind then. Just wondered

I wait for a reply, holding my breath in spite of myself. Maybe he'll ask again, press me into telling him why I wanted to know if he was available. Maybe I'll admit it – that I'm alone and missing Will and don't know what to do with myself. I think I remember Will saying that Harry has a troubled past with his family. Maybe he'll decide to come back to London early and raise a glass in Will's honour, even if I can't join in.

But as the minutes pass and Harry doesn't reply, the hope dwindles. I scroll up to the last text exchange we had and wince. I tried to warn him off Will back then, paranoid that Harry was trying to take him away from me. As it turns out, there *was* someone driving a wedge between us – but Harry was innocent. I never apologised. I don't blame him for not really wanting to hear from me.

I set the phone down on the coffee table beside me, losing all hope of it pinging with any new messages. Everyone I know is spending time with the ones they love – everyone but me.

And Will. He's also alone tomorrow, in an unfamiliar place with strangers. Maybe instead of wallowing, I can find a way to make his day better. I sit up sharply, infused with a new sense of purpose.

This is one thing I can do for him – and in the meantime, it might take my mind off how sorry I'm feeling for myself, and just how much of an edge I could take off with a drink.

FOURTEEN – WILL

I woke up on Christmas Day without any of the momentary confusion that you sometimes hoped for after bad news. It might have been nice to spend a minute not knowing, being lost in the dream that I last had, even imagining that I was home. But from the moment I was aware that I was awake, I was also aware that I was in an eating disorder rehab clinic, and Ram was at home without me, and it was Christmas Day.

And I couldn't help but think that it was probably going to be the worst Christmas Day of my life.

I dragged myself out of bed and dressed slowly, feeling the ache in my bones of the cold weather. That was one thing that came from the anorexia. Being old before my time. I wasn't supposed to have the joints of a sixty-year-old, but here I was. And it was all my own fault – I couldn't deny that.

But I could definitely be grouchy about it on Christmas Day.

I reluctantly pulled myself downstairs to the communal dining room, where the other patients were also gathering for breakfast. I took a bowl of porridge, which was at least warm and filling, and sat down to nurse it, not wanting to talk to anyone. Jake was there already, but he seemed as subdued as everyone else; he just nodded at me and carried on eating his cereal, staring at an empty spot on the table ahead of him. Probably missing his girlfriend, I guessed.

"Wallace." The grunted name at my ear made me start and turn around, seeing John at my elbow. He beckoned me furtively away, and I got up from the table to join him in the hall, away from earshot of anyone else.

"What is it?" I asked, suddenly worried. He wasn't going to have a go at me now, was he? I'd already had my telling off from Claire, such as it was. I figured I'd got away with it otherwise. I didn't want to have to deal with more, not on an already miserable Christmas Day.

"I've got something for you." John looked both ways down the hall, and then slipped a slim package out of his pocket and dumped it into my hand. "You'd better open it in your room. Keep it hidden for now."

"What is it?" I asked, staring at the package – wrapped in Christmassy paper – for a moment before slipping it into my waistband, where it sat flat against my stomach under my jumper.

"It's not from me," John said, with a touch of exasperation. "Look, someone was very eager to get you a present today, alright? Eager enough to bribe me a bit."

"Bribe you?" I gave John a raised eyebrow. What was he going on about? Was this... something from Ram?

John gave a short sigh of irritation and then turned around, jabbing a finger towards his back. I could only stare. He was wearing a plain black hoodie from the front – but from the back, a lurid swirl of colours picked out the logo of The Demonic Flames.

Ram's father's band.

"It's limited edition," John said. "Only a few hundred of them made. I tried to get one back when they first came out, but they sold out in seconds. Anyway, I got talking to your friend over text. Turned out we both had something the other wanted."

I curl my fingers against my stomach, feeling the outlines of the package beneath my clothes. He traded it for me. He managed to find a way to get the message through – today of all days. Tears come to my eyes and I have to blink them back, nodding quickly.

"Right, well, I'll go to my room," I said.

John nodded and let me go, for once not saying anything about the fact that I hadn't finished my breakfast.

In the privacy of my room, I savoured the present, holding it in my hands, marvelling at the fact that Ram had even wrapped something – let alone that he had wrapped it so neatly. It must have taken him ages to get it right. He didn't exactly have a lot of practice. The normal procedure was for him to hand me a carrier bag containing a gift he'd bought the night before, usually with the receipt and the price tag both still inside due to his forgetting to remove them. This was something else.

I slowly and reverently opened the paper, trying not to tear it. Inside was a slim, pocket-sized book – luckily, since that made it easier to smuggle. A guide to Victorian murders, a little tongue in cheek with period-suitable language and mock-up newspaper headlines based on real events. It was perfect. I loved it. I held it against my chest for a moment, wishing there was a way Ram could know how much I appreciated the gift.

There was a bookmark hidden inside – a slip of white card, looking like he'd cut it out of a box himself with slightly rough edges. On one side he'd written a message:

Now when I look at the moon I think of you, and the life-saving gift of water.

I tried without success to swallow down a lump in my throat. I was delirious back then, in the cell, when the same tiny square of window that let in the light of the moon also let in rainwater, the water that probably saved our lives. For a while I had thought I might have dreamt it: Ram pulling me over to lay beneath the water so I could drink it, then kissing my face, catching the drops that ran over my skin. It was a moment of ecstasy, even against the awful backdrop of our captivity and starvation.

When I look at the moon, I'll think of you, too.

I took some time to compose myself before I could go out again. I wondered how Ram was doing – if he had found my gift. If he liked it. Somehow, mine didn't seem as heartfelt in comparison. I had prepared it before all of this, of course. I didn't know then what was going to happen.

Christmas dinner was already being served in the dining area when I came out of my room and joined the group again. Everyone had opened my jars and there was a stack of badly-wrapped presents waiting for me, too – Christmas ornaments made out of left-over felt and pipe cleaners, bracelets made from beads, and from Jake, a handmade card folder with a skull painted on the inside to hold my research along with the origami crane.

I sat down reluctantly, taking a place next to Jake this time. We were partners in crime, after all, even if Claire gave us a disapproving glance as we elbowed each other over the Brussels sprouts sitting on the table.

There was a festive atmosphere, even if not everyone was happy about having to eat. I took the serving dishes as they were passed around and loaded my plate with peas, carrots, potatoes, and finally gave in to the turkey and ham, the cranberry sauce, the Yorkshire pudding filled with stuffing balls, the festive sausage, even the sprouts. I took a bite that incorporated a tiny piece of everything, a challenge to get it all on the fork, and grinned. The flavours were amazing, filling me with warmth, reminding me of past Christmas dinners, of feeling like I was home.

"Cheers, mate," Jake said, holding up a glass of warm spiced punch, something that John had made at home and brought in as a non-alcoholic answer to mulled wine. I clinked my glass against his and nodded.

"Cheers." We both drank, and I nudged him before leaning closer to talk quietly into his ear. "I got a message from my roommate."

"Yeah?" Jake's eyes lit up. "Did he like his present?"

I shook my head. "He didn't say. But he managed to get me a present smuggled in as well."

Jake grinned happily. "See. Told you."

"Told me what?"

"That he would love you when he saw your message." Jake glanced across the room, checking no one was watching us, before adding his own piece of news. "I got a text from Becca as well, through John. She told me Merry Christmas, and she's still waiting for me."

I clapped him on the shoulder. "That's great news!"

"Happy ending for both of us at the end of this, isn't there?" Jake asked, looking down at his plate. He didn't look afraid or sickened or angry when he looked at the food anymore, like he had when I first arrived. He looked down at it like it was a challenge, something to be defeated. Something to do in order to get his reward. "Light at the end of the tunnel."

"Yeah, there is," I said, thinking about Ram's message. Maybe it hadn't explicitly said that he loved me, or that he wanted to be together when I got out. We would have to cross that bridge when we came to it – it could still be months yet before I was able to see him again. But he had made a reference to a time when we were close, physically as well as mentally, and with a fairly romantic sentiment attached to it. I had hope. For now, that was enough.

That night, I lay in bed with the curtains open, letting the light of the moon wash over my body. I imagined that I was bathing in it, that it was healing me. I looked out through the panes of glass and angled my head until I saw it, and I locked my eyes onto that slim disc of light until I couldn't see anything else. Not the window, not the room I was stuck in, not the intervening distance. I pictured him laying right beside me.

I remembered the feel of his hand on my hand. The way his hair had fallen over his face when he climbed above me. At last, and most of all, I remembered his kiss. I remembered, and I closed my eyes. It wasn't much – only one memory. But it was enough to keep me together until I could see him again.

And then, I hoped, we would make many, many more.

15 – RAM

I dream of him, and when I wake up, I'm shot through with pain to realise that it wasn't real. That he isn't here. It's Christmas morning, and I'm alone. I don't know if I have ever felt it so keenly in my life.

I drag myself through to the living room out of habit rather than any real desire, making a coffee while wrapping myself in a black velvet robe instead of getting dressed. What's the point? I'm not seeing anyone today. I managed to track down and bribe the guy whose phone Will used last night, and it's at least a little warming to picture him getting my gift today. I hope he likes it. I hope the guy actually follows through with the trade and hands it over, come to think of it.

I open presents from Asra, Alex, and my parents, arrived by post earlier this week: a cosy jumper, a Swiss army knife, and a party game based around several chocolates with hidden chilli peppers, respectively. And then I'm done with all of my festivities. I don't see the point in eating Christmas dinner alone, given that I already had the meal with Asra and Alex. I think briefly about taking down the decorations now, but I feel too lazy. I wander into Will's room instead and lie down on his bed, looking up at the bare walls, trying to pretend I don't miss him so much it fucking hurts like a hole in my chest.

I think over his words from the message, replaying them one more time. I don't have to look them up: I memorised them ages ago. *I sleep and dream of time with you, This Christmas there's much I can't do, But know me, seek, and you will find, That you rest still inside my mind.*

What does it even mean? God, Will. Couldn't he have just told me?

I rest my head back onto his pillow and then freeze. This – this is the place where he sleeps and dreams. I thought that line was just a bit of an introductory section, something to get the rhyme going and tell me I'm on his mind, but –

Rest. I rest still inside his mind. And what do you do in bed? You rest. He didn't have the chance to pick out a clever hiding place. He'd already stashed it away when he left – the riddle is just a way to help me find it. I've been thinking about it too hard. The answer is obvious.

I throw myself over the side of the bed, landing on my knees on the floor, and cast about underneath it. There's something under there – a discarded scarf, which I left where it was last time I searched the room. I thought it might be dirty or gross, and there was a reason Will had shoved it under there.

Will, who never leaves a mess anywhere. His room has always been tidy and neat, no matter what the circumstances. By the time I'd managed to have a shower in our new place on the day we moved in, he'd put all of his belongings away so neatly it looked like a fucking show home.

Know me. And I do know him. Despite all the ways I've been kicking myself this week, I do. I know he would never intentionally just leave something a mess, no matter if it's just one thing.

I reach for the scarf and pull it towards me, and wrapped inside, I find a small gift box – complete with a ribbon in a neat bow holding the lid in place.

I stare at it and laugh in surprise, though the noise comes out more like a sob. Sitting back on his bed I cradle it in my hands: a perfectly wrapped present, prepared so far in advance that I can only shake my head. It's just so perfectly Will. It takes me a long moment to find the calm inside that I need to open it, my hands shaking as I pull the bow apart and let the ribbon drop, lifting the lid.

Inside is a black leather bracelet set with small silver beads in the shape of skulls, a knotted cord that fits my wrist just so. It's exactly the kind of thing I would pick out for myself. He knows me so well. I put it on and then admire it, holding it up to the light, running my hands over the cords. Will touched this, I think; he picked it out and boxed it up for me. For a moment I feel closer to him than I have in a long while.

I wipe the tears away from my face, sniffing and trying to gather myself together. Will doesn't need me to lose it, I remind myself. He needs me to be strong for him so that I can support him when he gets out of the rehab centre.

And I am strong. I really am. Today, this week, it's just a blip – and no wonder. I'm home alone at Christmas. It's an emotional time of year for anyone. I'm going to get through this, and then get back to normal, and the business will be fine. We'll be fine. We'll make it work. No matter what kind of support Will needs from me when he comes home, he'll have it.

I'm just about to put on some music and make myself something to eat when my phone rings, making me clear my throat and dig it out of the pocket of my robe. It's my Mum's number flashing up on the screen, and I answer it without hesitation this time. It's Christmas Day, after all.

"Hey, Mum," I say. "Merry Christmas."

"Merry Christmas, Julie!" she enthuses. No matter how many years I've been alive, she still refuses to stop using my childhood nickname. When I was a kid, my Dad didn't realise that in English culture, Julie sounds like a girl. He called me that, and then Mum did, and she still hasn't stopped. "Did you get our present?"

"I did, thanks," I say, getting up and wandering back to the living room, where the discarded wrapping paper still litters the floor.

"We didn't get anything from you," Mum says, her voice clearly hinting that she wants to know whether to expect anything or not.

"It's probably still stuck in the post," I say, making a mental note to get online and order something with fast delivery as soon as I put the phone down. "You know how it gets this time of year."

"Mmm," Mum agrees. "So, how's your friend? Will? Is he doing better yet?"

"Not yet," I sigh. "I don't know if you read about this in the papers, but he's gone into a longer-term programme for rehabilitation. The journalists thought it was because of the damage done by Coil, but – well, Will's been struggling for a while. He's getting some help."

"Does that mean you're alone?" Mum asks, her voice getting serious. "Julie, you should have said something! You know you're always welcome here!"

"I've got plans with friends," I lie.

"Oh, alright." Mum pauses. "Well, when's he coming back? You can come and stay with us if you want."

"I've got clients still here in London," I say, another lie, rubbing a hand over my forehead. She hasn't brought up the money yet. I wonder if she's going to. "Sorry, Mum, but I've got to stay. Life has to go on. When Will gets back, we'll be right back to normal – I can't let things lapse in the meantime."

"Alright then," Mum sighs. "I just miss getting visits from my baby boy. You've got to come and see us sometime this year. I don't want it to be next time you're in a hospital that we see you again."

"Alright, I will," I say. It's too reasonable a request for me to object to it – and besides, it's Christmas. I don't want to ruin her day by saying I really don't have any plans to go over there anytime soon, whether I owe Dad or not. "You're having a good day, though?"

"Oh, yes," Mum laughs. "Your Auntie Maren is here, and we dug out the chocolate fountain last night. It turns out you can put other things than chocolate in there. Isn't that funny?"

I hold back a groan, not wanting to either guess or find out what they might have got up to. "I'm glad you're having fun," I say instead, hoping that will put her off telling the story. "Love to Auntie Maren. I should get on, though."

"Oh, of course, sweet pea, I'm sure you've got lots to do," Mum trills. "See you soon, then."

"Yeah, Mum, see you soon," I say.

"Love you, Julie!"

With that, she puts the phone down, though I can hear her calling out to Maren even before the line goes dead. She didn't mention Dad once. I guess she thought it would be too touchy of a subject.

Well, at least that's over for another year, and it wasn't so bad. Looking down at my phone, I realise that I have messages from both Asra and Alex, wishing me a good Christmas. I fire off replies, smiling to myself. I guess I'm not so alone after all – there are people out there who care about me. It's been hard to remember that when the person I most want to be with is out of reach, but we'll get there again.

I sit and watch stupid reruns on television, eating Christmas-themed snacks, crackers cut into tree shapes and crisps that taste of cranberries and stuffing, letting the day wash over me and away. I get an early night to avoid the temptation of heading out to the off-license to see if it's open, and lay in bed with the curtains open so I can see the night sky, out above the roof of the apartment block opposite us.

It's lucky; right at this exact angle, in Will's bed, I can see the moon hanging like a silver disc above the city. A little obscured, sure, but it's there. I know I promised Asra I would sleep in my own bed, but today can't hurt. Just one night, feeling as though he's here with me, if I just close my eyes and pretend.

The light of the moon drenches me and I let my mind wander, remembering. The salt-sweet flavour of his lips that night. The way we kissed, I was so sure he wouldn't look back. Even if he ended up backing off that time, I won't let it happen again. I picture him laying beside me, try to imagine what I would say, what I would do.

This time, when I kissed him, I would make sure he knew I meant it. I would savour it, take it slow until he was gasping for more. And then I wouldn't give it to him. I would lay there and look into his eyes, and I would tell him I needed to know that it was real. And only when he told me it was would I dive in with both feet – give him my heart on a plate – when I knew he couldn't run away from me again.

But in the end, I know that's just a fantasy. The truth is, he already has my heart, whether I like it or not. And however long I have to wait to find out whether he still wants it, I will. Because even the pain of waiting is worth how it will be to have him in my arms again at last.

"Merry Christmas, Will baby," I whisper up at the moon, hoping that somewhere on the other side of London, just one moment of magic allows him to hear me.

READ MORE

Enjoyed this book? Then sign up for Rhiannon's mailing list at rhiannondaverc.co.uk – and get your hands on a free short story download!

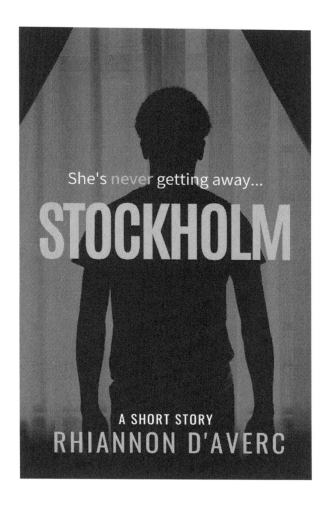

Subscribing also gets you release announcements and newsletter-only exclusives, including snippets from Will's case files, live event announcements, giveaways, free-to-read short stories, and more. Sign up now!

AND LAST BUT NOT LEAST…

"We appreciate every Amazon and GoodReads review, and read every single one. We'd love for you to leave your thoughts on this book!" – William Wallace

"And you'd better be fucking nice about it. Maybe tell everyone how fucking gorgeous I am, yeah?" – Julius 'Ram' Rakktersen

"…" – William Wallace

Follow the latest news…

Website - rhiannondaverc.co.uk

Twitter - twitter.com/rhiannondaverc

GoodReads - goodreads.com/author/show/16733877.Rhiannon_D_Averc

Amazon - http://author.to/rhiannon

Printed in Great Britain
by Amazon